DANGEROUS

DADDY

Little Lost #5

Charity Parkerson

Punk & Sissy Publications

Copyright

—Warning: This book is intended for readers over the age of 18. Some of my books contain allusions to past abuse and trauma.

CONTENTS

Introduction

*FOR THE FIRST TIME, **Adan is free. He's
happier than he's ever been. The past
doesn't care about any of that.***

Since Beau kicked Adan to the curb, leaving him homeless, Adan has been on a journey of finding himself. He spent his life on his knees and now he wants more. Adan has friends for the first time. Life is finally leaning his way. Unfortunately, Beau has other plans for Adan, and his newfound independence might not be as unconstrained as he believes.

After spending over a decade in prison, Axton has been floundering. He has friends who feel like family, but no goals or ambitions. Everything is different on the outside. He's not who he was ten years ago, and he doesn't know where to go with that. The only place he feels seen and accepted is with Adan. He understands Adan is a Little. Axton also knows he's no daddy. So far, that's stopped him from pursuing the only person who makes him feel. Unfortunately, he's not the only one with Adan on his radar and Adan might just need Axton's dangerous lack of conscience more than he needs a daddy. But protection is protection, as long as they don't end up dead, that is.

Dangerous Daddy is the fifth book in Charity Parkerson's Little Lost series where adorable, sometimes bratty, and scared Littles meet the men of their dreams.

Author Note

This series is a darker daddy/Little series. There's murder, suicide, and abuse along with heavy drug use. These are truly daddy/Little books with everything that entails. They won't be for everyone.

CHAPTER ONE

HE WAS THERE. JUST like every day. Different booth. Same soulless stare. No matter where Beau sat, Adan ignored him. He didn't serve him or look his way. Adan simply played a game inside his head: don't see the daddy. Then, when his shift ended, Adan would sneak from the back door and dart up the stairs to the safety of his apartment. Unfortunately, he would be trapped inside from that point until his boss, Wrecker, gave him the all clear. The entire situation was something out of a nightmare. It was Adan's life.

A different familiar face appeared in Adan's section. A smile exploded across Adan's face. He didn't hesitate to skip to Axton's side and slide into the booth across from him. The giant biker was one of the few people he could call his friend... maybe the only person who wasn't faking it.

"Hey." Adan sounded every bit as breathless as he felt.

A slow, sexy grin stretched Axton's lips. "Hey. Will you get in trouble for taking a break?"

Adan shook his head. "We're dead today and Wrecker is fine with some socializing, especially if it brings people back."

Axton's eerie light green eyes moved over Adan's face before sliding over his shoulder. He focused on Adan again. "He's still coming around."

It wasn't a question. Everyone was fully aware of Beau's stalking. There simply wasn't anything anyone could do. Beau was the biggest weapons dealer on the west coast. He was deadly. He was untouchable.

Adan shrugged. He tried to look unaffected. "All I can do is ignore him and hope he gets bored."

Axton worked a hair tie from his wrist and pulled his long, platinum blond hair into a bun. Everything about him was ethereal. His features were cut and too perfect. Only his pierced bottom lip and tattoos cut through the perfection, making him look real. He wasn't Adan's type at all, but he would never understand why the guy was single. Adan had never met anyone who gave off such a masculine vibe—like he should be scared, but also turned on. It was odd. But he was Adan's friend, and Adan counted himself lucky for that.

Adan fought to keep his smile. He was a bad person, and everyone knew it. He had never been sure why Axton didn't seem to care. "I'm always happy to see you. Are you doing okay?" He had to change the subject from Beau.

Axton didn't answer. "Meet me on the roof at eleven."

A genuine smile hit. "Okay." It was something they had discovered together. Well, Axton had shown up one night and, out of boredom, climbed a ladder on the backside of the building. After exploring, he had called for Adan to join him. It turned out there were lounge chairs and a table up there. Since that night, they had done a lot of stargazing together.

The door opened, and a crowd poured in. Adan blew out a sigh. "It looks like I need to get back to work. I'll see you tonight."

Axton dipped his chin.

Adan slid from the booth. He froze. "Oh. Can I take your order?"

A low, sexy rumble of laughter came from Axton's chest. "You know what I like."

With happiness and balance restored to his life, Adan bounced away to take more orders. Beau was still there. His gaze still followed Adan, but Adan wasn't alone anymore, and he wasn't the same child Beau had seduced. He wouldn't go back to being Beau's prisoner. As they say, a gilded cage is still a cage, and Beau's love killed people.

Since his release from prison, Axton spent more and more time at The PlayPen. It was a fetish club for daddy-Little relationships. Axton wasn't into any of that shit. He didn't judge either. No matter his disinterest, his friends were here. Axton watched them play with toy cars and smoke laced cigars. He did whatever they dragged him along to do. All Axton felt these days was a mild... nothingness, he supposed. Everything felt tepid. Maybe he was just used up.

Before his decade locked up, Axton went hard at everything. He partied too wild. Loved too much. Hated things he shouldn't. Ten years had given him time to reflect and see who the real ones were in his life. It was a lot fewer people than he expected, and the rest felt duty bound to stick by him.

"What are your plans tonight? Would you like to have dinner with Luca and me?"

Axton tried not to cringe at his brother's offer. He knew Jarek tried. It wasn't his fault Axton couldn't connect with him. Bitterness ran deep inside him.

"I have plans with a friend."

Jarek lasted all of two seconds. "I hope this isn't one of those friends who landed you in prison."

Axton didn't respond. He simply stared at Jarek with all the ambivalence he could muster

Jarek growled and shook his head. "Never mind."

Despite his best efforts, a hint of anger weaseled its way into his heart. He didn't want it. His rage served no one. He just wondered sometimes why Jarek was so blind. Axton knew he saw the differences between them. Jarek had as many years as Axton had to think about why they had turned out so differently. Jarek was a lawyer and perfect in every way. Dark hair and hazel eyes. He didn't wonder why Axton looked nothing like anyone in their family and had been treated like shit his entire life? Axton supposed he wouldn't. He had been the golden child, after all. Why would he notice Axton?

"It must be so nice to be you." Leaving things at that, Axton stood. He would head to Adan's early. Adan never judged him.

"Axton." Jarek sounded defeated. "Don't go. I wasn't trying to run you off. Forget I said anything."

The saddest part was, he saw his brother trying. He knew Jarek wanted a relationship. But something had died inside Axton a long time ago, and he didn't know how to change. Axton paused. He wished he knew what to say. It wasn't like he didn't want his brother. His gaze slid toward the spot where Jarek's husband sat nearby—on the floor and playing with blocks. He was adorable and not at all who Axton pictured capturing his brother. Luca's existence proved Jarek had a loving side. Unfortunately, no love had been extended to Axton by anyone in his so-called family, and it was too late to undo that damage.

Still, Axton cleared his throat. "It's not you. I told Adan I would meet him."

Jarek blinked—like Axton had slapped him. "Adan? As in Beau's Adan?"

Axton's hackles were all the way raised again. "He's not Beau's Adan. He's just Adan. People aren't property."

"In this case, they absolutely are," Jarek shot back. "Are you trying to get yourself killed? Because that's exactly where things are headed if you're messing with

Adan. Beau will definitely see you dead before he lets that guy go. Plus, what about Banks? He's supposed to be your friend."

"What about Banks?" Banks asked, appearing from nowhere and claiming the seat Axton abandoned.

Axton motioned Jarek's way. "He's angry because I'm going to meet Adan."

"Oh." Banks sounded completely unmoved. "Why?"

Jarek looked between them. His frustration couldn't be missed. "Why? Adan is the reason your mother took her own life. He's the reason your brother tried to kill himself."

There was some new information in there for Axton.

Still, Banks looked unruffled. "No, he's not."

"What do you mean, he's not?" Jarek looked more irritated by the second.

Banks shrugged. He was rarely bothered by anything. "Mom had a drug and alcohol problem. I'm sure seeing Adan with Dad didn't help anything, but she chose her addiction until she couldn't anymore. That's not Adan's fault. As far as Boone goes, it's possible he still sees things that way, and I guess Adan had a hand in things, but I can't believe you'd blame a child over the old man who seduced him." The way Banks held Jarek's stare said he expected more from Jarek. "And that's exactly what Adan was when my father put him on his knees." His hard voice almost made Axton take a step back. For all Banks' carefree attitude, he could also be terrifying. His gaze swapped to Axton. "Tell Adan he's still welcome here. I don't know if he's stopped coming around for our sakes or not, but it isn't necessary."

Without looking his brother's way, Axton dipped his chin and headed for the door. It was a little too early to meet Adan. He straddled his Harley and fired it to life. Because he was still the same terrible person who ended up doing time, he headed for the wrong side of town. Nothing good ever happened where he was going. But he wasn't good and there was no sense in pretending. Even his brother expected nothing less.

CHAPTER TWO

THE STARS WERE BRIGHT tonight, despite all the light pollution. Adan wondered all the time what the sky looked like in secluded areas. He had seen pictures and videos, but real life always beat reproductions. Adan had never been anywhere, except to hell. He twisted the tail on his pajamas and refused to go down that road. Adan did what he always did when he couldn't breathe. He thought about Boone.

Not the Boone who hated him now, but the one who had loved him. Adan imagined he was the only person who ever truly had. He recalled every second of the first time they met. Adan had been sassy. That was always how he dealt with being nervous. Adan shivered. He knew what he had lost, but Adan wasn't allowed to show it because it was completely his fault. Just like everything else, Boone was completely gone from him now. It was a bad mental health day. Not that he had good days.

"You look cozy."

Adan startled at Axton's sudden appearance. He had been so lost in his thoughts, he hadn't heard Axton's Harley approach. Adan looked down at his fuzzy pajamas—one of the few things he had been allowed to keep when tossed in the street. "Yeah. Sorry. I know you're not into the whole Little scene."

"Don't apologize." Axton filled the lounge beside him. "I'd never change who you are."

"Really? I would. Change who I am, I mean. Not you," he clarified.

Axton's light gaze locked on to him. His nose ring caught the light. Everything about him fascinated Adan. He was the opposite of everyone Adan had ever known—in looks, anyhow. Axton was just as dangerous and deadly as everyone who had ever been in Adan's life. But he definitely wasn't the clean-cut expensive suit guy Adan had been surrounded by for years, and it was strangely comforting. Those suit-wearing guys had murdered his soul.

Adan had to change the subject. "Do you mind if I'm extra nosey?"

Axton shrugged. He nodded toward Adan's open wine bottle. "Do you mind if I take a swig of that?"

"Go for it."

Adan watched as Axton dug out a baggie full of pills and fished out a couple. He washed them down with Adan's wine. Axton winced. "Shit. That's nasty." He held the bag out. "Do you want in on this?"

Curiosity always won. Adan leaned closer. It wasn't like he had anything going for him anyhow. He eyed the pills. "There's a lot of them. I wouldn't know what to take." But he wanted to. Just like with the wine, it was disgusting because Adan didn't know how to pick alcohol. Beau had never let him drink.

Axton shook the bag and eyed the inside. He hunted through the contents and found two white ones that looked alike. "Take these. They won't knock you out or have you bouncing off the walls. You'll just feel good."

That sounded amazing to Adan. He washed them down with the wine. It truly was gross. His tongue immediately loosened.

"Sorry. I didn't know which wine to pick. Wrecker's husband only recently took me to get my ID so I could buy alcohol. Beau never let me drink or anything. All the stuff Tabitha used to down is way out of my price range. Sorry. I shouldn't talk about them."

"You should stop saying you're sorry."

Adan fought the urge to say it again. Instead, he blurted out his question. "How did you end up in prison? I mean, I know you killed somebody, but what happened?"

Axton took another big swig of the nasty wine, as if he needed fortification. He swiped the back of his hand across his mouth. "How about we trade? I'll answer that one as soon as you tell me how you ended up with Beau."

Adan wanted to cringe, but it was a fair trade. He couldn't imagine prison was much better than Beau. His head spun a little. He leaned back and stared at the sky. The euphoric feeling that slowly overcame him made it easier to talk.

"I was young, dumb, and easily manipulated." A humorless laugh escaped him. He didn't want to relive the past, but it was all Adan saw as he explained. "Unfortunately, it didn't start with him. I grew up being my uncle's special little guy." Chill bumps rose on Adan's skin. If Axton didn't know what he meant, Adan couldn't explain. There weren't enough drugs in the world for that story. "I became someone I'm not proud of, but I survived. Then I met Boone." A smile tugged at the corners of his mouth, just picturing Boone and the way he had felt safe for the first time in his life. "I thought I had won the jackpot. He still lived with Beau back then. I practically lived there too, spending as much time as I could away from home. His house felt like home to me." It truly had, and he fucking hated that now.

Adan swallowed his bitterness and continued. "Since Boone works for his dad, he had to run errands a lot. It was pretty common for me to hang around even when he wasn't there. We had a fight. It was so stupid, I don't even remember what it was about. Probably me being a bitch." A humorless laugh fell from Adan's lips. "Anyhow, it wasn't a quiet fight. There was no need to be discreet since Beau and Tabitha were screaming and throwing shit at each other. Truthfully, Boone's anger was probably due to their antics. Not that it matters now."

Adan drew his knees up and wrapped his arms around them, trying to make himself smaller. "Beau stormed into the room, looking thunderous. He barked for

Boone to get the fuck out and get to work. Tempers were high all around, but Boone left. When he was gone, I don't know what happened, really. Beau kind of bitched about me always being there. I got bitchy right back, and he laughed. He transformed into someone I had never seen before."

He finally looked Axton's way. "I know you've done some work for Beau, but do you know him? Like, have you ever truly sat and talked to him?"

Axton shook his head.

Adan held his stare. He needed Axton to understand this part, if nothing else. "He's terrifyingly larger than life. When you sit with him, it's like watching a cobra dance. You know he could strike any second and you'll be dead, but you can't look away. Even when he smiles, maybe especially when he smiles, you're in serious danger." He looked away and went back to watching the stars. "There's no soul inside him. What he felt for Tabitha and what he feels for his sons, it isn't love. It's possessiveness—like a dragon and its hoard. Once he makes a decision, everyone has to fall in line and play their part to perfection. He doesn't consider anyone else's feelings because he has none. Beau enjoys nothing more than to throw the L word around because he doesn't know the difference between ironclad control and adoration. So when he told me I now lived there permanently and I would never return to the horrible life I had known, I only had one other choice besides doing as told. I could die because there was no way he could make that decision and risk me telling Boone if I said no. It was one thing to break his son while telling himself he had to have me. It was a whole other for Boone to learn he tried to take me, and I refused. I don't expect you to understand that. You're not like him. But I understood, because maybe I sort of am like him. I broke Boone and sold my soul. The worst part is, I think—at the time—I wanted it. He was the most powerful person I had ever encountered. I knew no one would dare touch me again."

He looked Axton's way again. A bitter smile tugged at his lips. "Like I said, young and stupid. At the time, I didn't understand that death could sometimes be better. But make no mistake, I played that role. For ten years, I smiled and flirted. Got on my knees. I stood where I was told to stand and laughed when told to laugh.

I've been a puppet for so long, I have no idea who I am, but I lived. I survived."

"Jarek says you're the reason Boone tried to kill himself."

Adan's wince came from his soul. He looked away and sipped his wine. No one could know how much Adan hated Axton knowing that part. "Yeah. I thought Beau would toss me out back then, but Boone survived, and it was like Beau had to double down. He had to love me, or he had destroyed his son for nothing. So Beau claimed to love me, and I—" Adan swiped his sweaty palms on his thighs. "So, how did you end up in prison?" He couldn't talk about himself any longer or the destruction he had caused. Adan already had to live with the pain. He didn't think he could handle Axton looking at him differently.

"I was young and dumb and didn't realize there were worse fates than death."

They shared a smile. It was ridiculous. The moment shouldn't have been funny, but it kind of was. Adan felt ridiculously close to Axton sometimes. They were so different, yet alike.

Axton broke the spell. He shook his head and looked away. "I ran with this biker gang. Don't ask me how I got mixed up with them. It was a series of too many small things to recount. Things were bad at home. They were there, giving me an unhealthy outlet. I got pretty heavy into drugs and even deeper into their bullshit."

A bitter smile touched Axton's lips. He looked Adan's way. "It was everything you see in the movies except worse. They told me I had to kill a guy, so I did." He said the words so casually—like a life meant nothing and then kept going. "My brother is a damn good lawyer, but even he couldn't save me completely. He got my charges reduced to manslaughter. I still got a massive sentence, but I was supposed to only serve seven years. Then I just couldn't stay out of trouble and they kept tacking on time. So when I was asked to kill someone else in exchange for my freedom, I did. A murder landed me behind bars, and another saved me. So yeah, I get how you couldn't say no. Beau wanted me to kill a snitch before the guy could testify against his family. For me, it was a no brainer. Saying yes to Beau saved me too. Maybe not my soul," he said with a bright smile that was obviously fake. "But that was a lost cause anyhow."

Yeah. As fucked up as it was, he felt closer to Axton than anyone. His gaze moved over the hair so light, it looked almost unnaturally white in the moonlight. Cold-blooded killer or not, he was grateful Axton was here. Maybe bad people always found each other. Whatever the reason, Adan was thankful for the company at the bottom. Even if he had a choice, Adan would still choose Axton for company. Like recognized like.

Axton saw what Beau had seen in Adan. The guy had a spark. He was beautiful and just the right amount of bitter. Someone like Beau would take one look at Adan and see someone he could twist and bend. He looked too caustic to break. Everything about that would speak to a monster like Beau. There was no sport in crushing a weak man. He wondered if Beau thought he had won now. Unfortunately, Axton had a bad feeling Beau wanted Adan twice as much. That was a deadly spot for anyone in Adan's sphere. Luckily, Axton should have died a long time ago, and he wasn't the least bit scared. He had killed for Beau. He could kill Beau too.

"You feeling those pills yet?"

Adan cocked his head, as if thinking over Axton's question. "Oddly, no. I only feel a slight buzz. That could be the wine."

"Something more powerful it is." He picked through the bag again and passed Adan two more pills. "If you pass out, I don't know how easy it'll be to carry you down the ladder."

Adan tossed the pills back without inspecting them. After polishing off the wine and swallowing the pills, Adan stood. "Let's go inside, then. I bought a different bottle of something or another. We can open that and see if I die." The way Adan smiled proved he wasn't opposed to the idea.

"I'd be sad if you died, so maybe don't do that." He stood and followed Adan down the ladder. Together, they headed inside Adan's tiny apartment. Adan made his way to the kitchen, and Axton stayed on his heels. He didn't know why. Axton just liked being in Adan's company. He wanted to enjoy as much of Adan's time as he could get.

Adan pulled a bottle of Jack out of the fridge.

Axton laughed at the sight of it. He didn't think Adan would handle that well at all, but he couldn't wait to see.

At his laugh, Adan turned and bumped into Axton's chest. He eyed Axton's body, blinking. He laughed.

It occurred to him Adan was more fucked up than he realized.

Adan chuckled again. "You're just so fucking big."

A smile exploded across Axton's face.

Adan didn't stop there. "You just take up so much space. My apartment feels even smaller." He cocked his head and met Axton's stare. "It's just occurred to me I don't know what your place looks like. Is it built for a giant?"

He wasn't quite that big. "Would you like to see my place?"

"Sure." He set the bottle aside and pressed his hand against his forehead. "Whoa. Maybe not tonight, though."

Axton couldn't stop smiling. He couldn't explain why he was having so much fun, but he hadn't been this happy in a long time. Maybe it was because Adan officially knew him better than anyone and still wanted to be around him.

Adan swayed.

Axton jumped into action. "I've got you." He swept Adan off his feet.

A loud laugh burst from Adan. "Wow. Big and strong."

Axton shook his head. "Where are we headed? The couch or the bed?"

For a moment, Adan stared up at him—like having an existential crisis.

An uncomfortable laugh escaped Axton. They were simply standing there, and he wasn't sure Adan hadn't checked out.

His laughter seemed to shake Adan from his frozen state. "Do you want to take me to bed?"

It was Axton's turn to internally panic. He didn't know the right answer. Did he want to take Adan to bed? That obviously wasn't what he meant, but Adan had asked, and now Axton didn't know how to answer. Adan was beautiful, and Axton liked him better than most people. It was possible Adan's whole Little thing had stopped him from seeing Adan sexually, but now that he had been asked directly, he couldn't say he didn't want Adan. Fuck. Did he want Adan? He smelled good, and Axton was always ridiculously happy to see him. In fact, Axton woke up every day and plotted excuses to see him. Goddamn. He wanted the guy.

Axton shook his head, coming back to himself. As he focused on Adan, a chuckle escaped him. He was dead to the world. "Bed, it is."

He headed for the bedroom. It was a mess. Axton wasn't surprised. Adan seemed very chaotic. The unmade bed made it easier for Axton to tuck him beneath the covers. For a moment, he simply stared at Adan, trying to figure out what he should do now. Adan looked kind of overheated. He uncovered him. There. The kitty pajamas should be enough. He gently removed the kitten ears headband and set it aside.

With nothing left to do, Axton moved through Adan's apartment, doing everything he would before going to bed at home. He made Adan a glass of ice water and left a few Tylenol next to it. With that out of the way, he found Adan's phone and plugged it in. He pulled out his phone and texted Adan so he would see it in the morning.

Axton: *Fucking lightweight, I showed myself out. If you're serious about seeing my place, I'll see you tomorrow night at six. You'll probably be reading this tomorrow, so tonight. Six. 1436 Shoreline Rd. If you can't make it, let me know. Fuck. You don't have a ride. Change of plans. I'll be here at six. If you don't want to come, let me know before then.*

Axton stared at his rambling text. None of that was necessary. He hit send nonetheless and then laughed at himself. It had been like five minutes since he decided he wanted to fuck Adan and he was already a mess. Goddamn. The entire situation was just dumb as hell. He had no plans to stop.

CHAPTER THREE

THEY WERE ALONE. IT was like something out of Adan's nightmares. Wednesdays were always dead, but this was insane. Beau sat in the corner. Adan tried desperately to ignore the eyes that followed his every move. He wiped down counters and swept nonexistent crumbs. More than once, Adan considered calling Wrecker and pleading for help, but he couldn't put anyone else in danger.

"You'll get that boy killed."

Nothing else could have pulled a response from Adan. Adan's head shot up and his gaze locked with cold brown eyes. He refused to be weak. "Which boy? You'll have to be more specific."

"Don't play dumb. Axton owes his freedom to me. I'd hate for him to turn up dead now."

Adan should have seen this coming. That didn't make it hurt less. He would keep Axton safe but knowing that was his only choice hurt. The pain made him lash out. "How pathetic you must be to need to kill someone to stop any chance of competition."

Beau leaned back and eyed him. "So you are fucking him."

A pain bloomed between Adan's eyes. He pinched the spot, hoping to ease the pressure. "I'm not fucking anyone." He dropped his hand. "Why do you care anyhow? It's not like we were ever real."

"You know that's not true. I love you."

Adan snorted so hard, it hurt. "This isn't what love looks like, Boo." Adan wanted to bite off his tongue. The nickname he had always used for Beau when they were alone rolled so easily off his tongue. Beau's triumphant expression made him want to puke. At least he hadn't accidentally called him Daddy.

"You've always been fanciful. True love looks ugly more often than you think."

He was so goddamn tired. "I don't want your ugly love." Even Adan heard the exhaustion in his voice.

"I don't remember you having complaints when you were getting everything you wanted."

Adan held his stare. "When was that? It seems to me you bought a lot of things for you. Otherwise, I wouldn't have spent several weeks homeless. I wouldn't have been forced to scrounge for food and hide just so I could sleep. You didn't give me anything except pain."

Beau shocked him. "You're right. I wasn't exactly thinking straight after finding Tabitha. You didn't deserve the way I treated you. I can't go back in time, but I can fix things now. Just come home. All your things are still waiting for you."

There was so much sitting on Adan's chest. He was terrified he couldn't escape. His future unfolded before his eyes, and it was nothing but years and years of being seen as nothing but property. He wanted to cry. Adan wouldn't give Beau the satisfaction.

"I want to be loved. For real." The confession fell from Adan's lips, sounding every bit as desperate as he felt. "I don't want to be the weapon you use to bludgeon your family. The thought of spending the rest of my life as nothing, while you still do whatever you want with whomever you want, all while knowing I could be out in the streets with nothing again at any time. That sounds like hell. I'd rather be dead."

"I can arrange that."

Adan didn't back down. He didn't flinch. "Then do it."

The door opened and a party of six poured in, followed by three more people. Adan focused on taking orders while ignoring Beau. He hated his thoughts. The thing was, coerced or not. Manipulated or not, Adan had spent ten years of his life with Beau. They hadn't all been bad. Sometimes, they would go months where Beau made him feel like he was the most precious thing in the world. Adan would start to think maybe they were real. Maybe Beau had finally given up on Tabitha and accepted the drugs and alcohol had won. Possibly, he loved Adan for real and he could find some happiness in the situation. Every single time, Tabitha would do or say something that had hope surging inside Beau again. Then Adan was back to playing a role. Beau's touches and glances turned fake again. Now there was nothing left of Adan but an empty shell. He hadn't been much more than that to begin with.

Adan had done so many terrible things. He had no excuse. Adan had simply been trying his damnedest to feel anything except the pain and shame he had dealt with for as long as he could recall. He had done everything, hoping someone would love him for real. Adan felt sick every time he thought about the victims he'd left in his wake, as he tried like hell to heal. He was a bomb of trauma. But he was an adult now, and he refused to be that person again. Axton had listened to his story and hadn't judged him. Adan had woken up after their night together full of hope and horribly hungover. He regretted nothing. Now Beau was saying Adan would have to cut ties or watch him die. Adan knew there was only one real choice. He would have to let Axton go. But Axton deserved to hear it in person. Adan wouldn't be a coward. He would tell Axton the truth and thank him for his friendship. Adan wouldn't leave another body in his wake. For once, Adan needed to put someone else first. No matter how much it shattered him.

Axton was oddly nervous. He had spent the day cleaning before showering and heading out to get Adan. To his surprise, Adan sat outside on the staircase leading to his apartment. He stood, twisting his fingers as Axton approached. A bad feeling overcame him. He wouldn't spend his night guessing what he had done wrong.

Axton didn't even bother greeting him. "What's wrong?"

A sad smile touched Adan's lips before falling away. "I spoke to Beau today."

Axton's stomach dropped. It had never occurred to him Adan might eventually go back to Beau, but why wouldn't he? Cruelty aside, he could give Adan the world. "Oh."

A genuine smile snapped to Adan's lips. "What's that oh about?"

Axton shrugged. "What happened?"

Adan's happiness vanished. He went back to twisting his fingers. "He said I'd get you killed."

Axton nearly laughed. He had been waiting for Beau to play that card. Without a word, Axton plucked the cat ears from

Adan's head. He unzipped his leather jacket and stuffed them inside. "I'll keep these safe," he promised as he re-zipped his jacket. "Now." He grabbed the extra helmet he had hooked on his bike. "Let's get this on you."

"Ax—"

Axton plopped the helmet on Adan's head, cutting off his argument. He didn't speak until he worked to tighten the helmet. "I'm not afraid." He paused and held Adan's stare for a moment. "Look into my eyes and tell me I'm lying." He let a second pass before he went back to adjusting Adan's strap. "Life hasn't managed to kill me yet and I won't give up my best friend over a threat from someone who wasn't even brave enough to make it directly."

"Are you being serious?" Adan sounded so lost, yet hopeful at the same time.

"Get on." Axton helped Adan climb on behind him. "Hold on. Don't let go."

"Okay." Adan sounded a little nervous.

Axton couldn't help but laugh when he took off and Adan squealed. His grip tightened on Axton. He hit Beach Road and opened her up, enjoying the laughter that poured through the speaker inside his helmet.

"We're almost there."

He felt Adan startle. "I heard you—like inside my helmet. Can you hear me?"

"Yep. Hold on. I'm about to turn down a sandy road."

Adan somehow managed to scoot even closer.

Axton had to take a breath. Now that he saw the truth about them, he couldn't stop thinking about having Adan beneath him. His bungalow came into view. Axton slowed and turned into his driveway. His garage door opened, and he slipped inside before the door closed behind him.

He helped Adan off the bike and then out of his helmet. "Here." He held Adan still and put his ears back on. Axton didn't know the story behind why Adan always wore them, but he was adorable. His dark curly hair matched the color of the ears to perfection. They almost looked real. Between the ears and his perfect green eyes, he could be a cat.

Adan's gaze never wavered from Axton's face. "Am I really your best friend?"

"Of course. Why do you think I can't stay away?"

"I've never been anyone's friend. At least, I don't think I have. Mostly, people either hate me, tolerate me, or use me."

That was the saddest thing Axton had ever heard, and he got it. Life hadn't been kind to either of them. "Well, now you can't say that."

Adan shifted from one foot to the other. "Can I see your house now? The garage is cute."

A laugh burst from Axton. Adan was unique. "Come on." He headed inside with Adan on his heels. The door inside the garage led into the laundry room. From there, they stepped into the kitchen. Axton peeled off his jacket and draped it over the back of a chair at the dining room table. "Feel free to look around."

While looking nervous and unsure of how free he actually was, Adan slowly walked through the house.

Axton followed him. The place wasn't huge. It was nothing like the luxury he had been raised in, but Axton didn't want that life—not that it was open to him. His parents had passed when Axton was in prison. They had left everything to Jarek. When Axton had been released, Jarek had used some of the money for this house. He had gotten Axton set up with a new life. It had taken a few months of staying out of trouble, but Jarek had eventually passed some of his inheritance to Axton. Jarek claimed he would eventually make sure Axton got half, but he needed to make sure Axton wouldn't use the funds to destroy his life. On one hand, Axton didn't think he was entitled to anything. On the other, the people who raised him absolutely owed him for every day he had spent in hell.

Adan ran his fingertips along the back of Axton's leather couch before heading down the hall. He poked his head inside the bathroom before eyeing Axton's home gym.

"Weights. I'm unsurprised."

Axton had no idea what that meant, but it still made him smile.

Adan passed the empty bedroom and paused outside Axton's room. He flashed

Axton a smile. "It looks exactly how I thought."

Axton eyed the room. Black covers and curtains matched the dark furniture. Everything was fairly new. "How do you mean?"

While wearing a sweet smile, Adan leaned against the doorframe. His smile slipped a hair. "I've never told anyone the things I told you last night."

That didn't surprise Axton. "Okay."

"I guess I'm trying to say you're my best friend too."

Fuck. Every second that passed, Axton wanted him even more. "Can I kiss you?"

Adan didn't look anywhere near as shocked as Axton felt. While Axton couldn't believe he had said that, Adan looked completely relaxed. His gaze moved over Axton's face. "You want to kiss me?"

"Yes." He would be damned if he backed down now.

"I've never kissed anyone with a lip ring. Won't that hurt?"

"No. I'd think you'd be more concerned over the tongue ring."

A smile snapped to Adan's lips. He straightened. "Your tongue is pierced? I've never noticed. Let me see."

Everything inside Axton relaxed. He realized this was what he adored about Adan. Axton wasn't uncomfortable at all. He was his realest self with Adan. Axton tried not to laugh as he stuck out his tongue.

"Oh, wow. How have I never seen that? A nose ring, lip ring, and now a tongue ring. I know your ears are pierced. How many piercings do you have?"

Axton shrugged. "I lost count."

Adan's eyebrows rose. "Let me see."

A smirk touched Axton's lips. "Are you sure about that?"

The innocent shock in Adan's expression made the moment worthwhile.

He decided to change the subject before he scared Adan. "Are you avoiding my question?"

A bark of laughter burst from Adan. He blushed. "Sorry. No. I got distracted and forgot." To Axton's surprise, Adan gripped his shirt and lured him down.

Axton's throat went dry. He didn't know what to expect, but it was anything and everything other than what he got. Adan was the aggressor. Once their lips met, Axton was the one holding on for dear life. Their tongues battled. Axton had Adan backed against the doorframe and still Adan was in charge. He blatantly inspected Axton's piercing. His hands ended up beneath Axton's shirt, as if he had to feel Axton's body. His fingertips skimmed Axton's nipples. Axton was so fucking hard, it hurt.

Adan's mouth moved to Axton's neck. "Not there," he said, caressing Axton's unpierced nipple again. He sucked Axton's skin while his hands slid south. Axton fought for his life, keeping his hands respectfully on Adan's hips, while Adan unbuttoned and unzipped his pants. His hand slid down Axton's dick, exploring each piercing. Axton panicked a little. Adan had him so turned on. He worried he might accidentally blow.

"I'd planned to cook you dinner."

Adan immediately took a step back, as if nothing had happened. "Okay." He sounded chipper and entirely too unaffected for Axton's pride.

Axton overcame Adan. His every thought scattered. If he had ever possessed an ounce of good sense, it vanished. With the temptation breaking him, Axton snapped. He snatched Adan from his feet. The bed was too close. It took nothing to be on top of him, inching closer to relief from this madness. He wasn't supposed to want someone like Adan.

Adan turned his head. "I'm pretty sure I started things, but I don't think I can do this."

Even though a roar of denial rang through Axton's head, he still rolled away. "It's okay. I didn't plan this."

"I know." Adan sniffed.

Axton turned his head in time to watch the first tear fall. Great. Now he felt like a bastard. "I'm sorry." He was so stupid. Adan wasn't like him. He was probably scared as hell now. Axton had gotten too rough.

Adan sniffed again. "Don't apologize. That's worse."

Now Axton was just confused. "Okay. Sorry. I've spent a majority of my adult life on the inside. I don't know how..."

Axton's hands rose and fell. He stared at the ceiling. His anger with himself grew. They never should have let him out. Every second, he got closer to spiraling. He didn't know how to exist among normal people.

Adan moved his arm and slipped beneath it. He rested his head on Axton's chest. "I spent all of my adult life a prisoner too. Just in a different way. I don't know how to build anything healthy and you're all I have. If I screw up and you go away, I'm scared of what I'll do. It's possible you're all that's keeping me from going back to Beau just so I'm not alone. Even though, logically, I know I was more alone than ever with him."

Adan was always so damn open with Axton. Axton felt like he needed to be the same. "I feel something for you." The admission was easy because it was Adan. Axton couldn't stop. "The night Tabitha died, and you left with me, I think that was the first time I had seen someone look on the outside the way I've felt on the inside my entire life."

Adan's head shot up. "I was totally shattered that night. Why would you feel like that? I thought Jarek and you came from a wealthy family with parents who stayed married until the day they died. That sounds nice."

Axton held Adan's stare. "They died in a car accident when my dad purposely drove them into the lake. It seems they were fighting. Someone overheard them at the party they had attended that night. They said my parents were yelling while waiting for the valet. My dad screamed about being sick of the same fight, being sick of her. I was the only fight they ever had because I'm the product of an affair. Jarek doesn't know," Axton tacked on before he could ask.

Adan didn't look surprised. "I wondered why Jarek and you look so much different."

A smile exploded across Axton's face. "Then you're a step ahead of Jarek." His smile fell. "Jarek was given everything. He was their golden child. Jarek didn't even notice the abuse I suffered. We might've both gotten all the same advantages, but it was all for show. My parents were all about appearances. For a long time, I thought if I made them proud, then they would love me. I never stood a chance. Life either makes you or breaks you." Axton swallowed. It hurt. "I'm pretty sure it's broken me."

Adan went back to cuddling against Axton's chest. "Well, look at us. Just a pair of fucked up people who went searching for love in all the wrong people."

Adan was right. Axton had ended up in the wrong crowd searching for love and acceptance. He hadn't realized he was only being used until it was too late. Axton had been so fucking angry back then, it probably wouldn't have mattered even if he knew. Being used was at least attention. Loneliness fucked with people's heads.

"I love you. I've never been this scared to lose anyone."

Axton blinked. It wasn't exactly a flinch. More of a shock than anything. No one loved him, but he couldn't deny Adan's words. He cleared his throat. "Yeah. I guess that's those feelings I talked about having for you too. Even though I know I'm not good at being human, and I don't know how to be whatever you need as a Little, you're all I think about. All my time is spent plotting ways to be with you."

Adan went up on to one elbow. "Is it okay if I kiss you again? I don't want to be a tease or anything, but—"

Axton grabbed the back of Adan's head and pulled him in for a kiss, cutting off his words. He didn't give a fuck about sex. While he very much wanted to be inside Adan, he wanted this more. A connection.

"Tell me about the cat ears," Axton demanded between kisses.

Adan chuckled against his lips. "They're cute. I wear them when I'm scared and need a confidence boost."

Axton held Adan away for a second so he could hold his stare. "I've never seen you without them."

"That's because I'm always scared."

Axton reclaimed Adan's mouth. They would be afraid together and figure this out. Their feelings were out there now. Everything else would eventually fall into place.

CHAPTER FOUR

RAIN POURED DOWN, SOAKING the city. It wasn't often Axton had to park his bike and take his truck instead. He was especially bummed about it today. Axton had promised Adan he would take him for a ride tonight. Starting out breaking his promises was definitely a bad look, but he couldn't control the weather.

He had time to kill before Adan got off work, and he was bored off his ass. Axton drove to a historic area near Adan's work where several boutiques were located. Most were locally owned and had an eclectic mixture of things for sale. He knew he could park, walk the covered sidewalk, and kill time. One of these days, he probably needed to stop living off his inheritance and get a job or something. The jobs willing to hire a felon weren't occupations he could see himself doing. Mostly, though, he was savoring his freedom. He wasn't ready to be trapped by a nine to five.

Axton roamed a few shops. Nothing caught his eye. Finally, at the store at the end of the block, he hit pay dirt. He spotted a bright yellow raincoat with matching duck boots. A smile lit his face as he grabbed the items and made his way to the register. While waiting for his transaction to clear, Axton glanced around.

His gaze landed on a mirror behind the register when the bell above the door jingled. One of Beau's henchman came in.

"Do you have a restroom?"

The twenty-something blond behind the counter eyed him. Lust tinted her features. He might have rolled his eyes if he wasn't attempting to stop a shootout in her shop. Axton got it. He looked like a dude who just got out of prison. For whatever reason, people thought that was hot. People were dumb.

"I'm not really supposed to let customers use our bathroom, but since you bought something." Her smile turned even more predatory. "It's down the hall."

He dipped his chin in thanks and slipped down the hallway unnoticed. Axton bypassed the restroom and found the back door. He took a breath. Fuck, he hoped it didn't have an alarm. He pushed it open and released his breath when no blaring sounds erupted. Axton made his way around the building to the corner, keeping an eye out for Beau. He wasn't scared of the guy. The number one rule of survival was to let no one take him to a secondary location, and there was no way Beau intended to confront him here. As he peeked around the corner, he spotted Beau's vehicle. The guy who had entered the store walked back out. His hands rose and fell, showing he had nothing. Axton watched him climb back inside the SUV. It slowly backed away. Thankfully, it headed in the opposite direction. The moment it was out of sight, he made for his truck. Axton wasn't stupid enough to start it right away. He checked the obvious places for any sign of trackers or explosive devices. Axton didn't put anything past Beau. As far as Axton was concerned, every move Beau made was dumb as hell. If he hurt Axton, Adan would never take him back. But Axton didn't think Beau had exactly been thinking clearly since Tabitha's death.

When he found nothing, Axton headed for the coffee shop. There was a good chance that was exactly where Beau was headed too, but Axton had the advantage this time. When the Back Porch came in to view, he immediately spotted Beau's SUV. Axton circled the building and parked by Adan's apartment. He checked his watch. Adan got off in five minutes.

Axton: *I'm here. Meet me out back when you're free.*

Adan: *Yay! Okay. I'm almost ready.*

If Beau wanted to confront him, he would do so in front of Adan. This wouldn't be some divide-and-conquer bullshit. While he waited, Axton removed the tags from his purchase. He wanted to be ready. When he spotted Adan running from the back door, dodging the rain, he threw open his truck door.

"I've got you."

Adan changed directions and darted into his arms.

Axton easily pulled Adan into his lap and out of the rain.

Adan was all smiles and laughter. "I got wet."

Axton couldn't stop smiling. He looked like a drowned cat. His curls were all over the place. "I've got just the thing." He handed Adan his haul.

Adan's eyes lit. "Oh my gosh. It's so cute." His voice took on the same tone as someone squishing a dog's face.

"Try them on. There's a bunch of puddles out here that have your name on them."

With an adorable giggle, Adan scrambled out of his shoe**s.** He put on the boots and Axton helped him into the jacket. He took off the cat ears and pulled up the hood before setting him back on the ground.

Axton swatted his ass. "Go have fun."

While wearing a huge grin, Adan ran for the biggest puddle. He dove in with both feet, stamping and sending water flying. Axton couldn't stop smiling. Adan looked his way, laughing. He stamped his way to another puddle.

Axton slipped from the truck and headed for the awning. He leaned against the building, staying out of the rain while still enjoying the show. Adan's childlike happiness was infectious. He had forgotten what it was like to savor the small things.

"I thought this wasn't your thing."

Axton startled at the sudden appearance of Boone at his side. Beau's oldest was a huge guy. He was also quiet, and Axton had never been able to get a read on the guy. His dark eyes, hair, and beard made him look hard and impenetrable. He had married a Little and seemed beyond gentle with him. But in every other aspect of life, Boone wasn't approachable.

He refused to let Boone see he had gotten the drop on him. "It's not."

"Mhmm." In one sound, Boone called Axton a liar in three languages.

"What are you doing here?" Axton didn't want to beat around the bush. He wanted to enjoy his day with Adan.

"I came with Dad to make sure he didn't kill you. He'd like to speak with you."

Axton kept his gaze locked on Adan and snorted.

"You know he won't let Adan go, right? If he wouldn't do it to save his relationship with me, there's zero hope for you."

"I'm not worried."

"You should be."

Axton turned his head. He held Boone's stare and let him see the killer he tried to keep hidden. "I'm not worried. Unlike your dad, I don't send others to do my dirty work."

Boone gave him a sharp nod. He cast a quick glance Adan's way. Adan laughed and stamped a path through the parking lot. "You make a good daddy. Adan deserves that."

That shocked the absolute fuck out of Axton. "I'd expect you to be the last person to say that."

Boone nodded. He looked thoughtful. "A year ago, you would've been right. When Mom passed, she left each of us a letter. Mine had a lot of thoughts on Adan. He's the same age as Banks. I'll admit, back then, I hadn't really thought about that since I'm not much older than him. But Mom, his age, is one of the biggest things she couldn't live with. Don't get me wrong; Mom hated him, but she wasn't unaware of his age or circumstances. She saw more in that house than she let on. She had a lot of reasonable things to say that I admit I hadn't considered. For one, seeing her husband with someone the same age as their youngest child made her worry she was married to a child molester. It ate at her, wondering if Dad had wanted Adan before he turned eighteen. If he was the first one. On the other hand, she knew Adan was just a weapon he used to destroy her. She had a lot going on and too many things she couldn't live with anymore. As someone who's tried to end it all." He motioned toward the scar on his head. "I understand her better than most. I get having all hope stripped away by the people you thought loved you the most. That's more on my dad's head than Adan's." A bitter-looking smile touched Boone's lips. "Not that I forgive anyone at all."

A soft chuckle escaped Axton. He fully understood bitterness. He sighed. "Look, I know Beau wants his toy back. I also know he won't stop. But what would you do if it was your husband he had his sights set on? Would you let him take a second man from you?"

The deadly shadow that settled into Boone's eyes reminded Axton of Banks at his most terrifying. "He wouldn't live to see tomorrow."

Axton dipped his chin. "Then you have your answer. This won't end well for one of us unless one of us backs down. It won't be me." He glanced Adan's way. Adan was frozen, standing in a puddle and staring at them. His face had bleached white. "Now, if you'll excuse me. I have a little one who needs me." Axton darted out into the rain. Adan watched him approach. He looked like he might be sick. Axton pasted on a bright smile and snatched Adan from his feet. He tossed Adan over his shoulder and spun. A squeal rent the air, turning Axton's smile genuine. Boone disappeared. Axton chose love.

Despite his new rain jacket and boots, they were both completely soaked by the time Adan let them into his apartment. Each time they looked each other's way, they burst into laughter. Axton had mud on his cheek. He looked adorable. Adan kept a tight grip on his hand as they toed off their shoes. He didn't let go as he dragged him toward the bathroom.

"I don't have anything your size." He fired the shower to life.

Axton peeled off his shirt. "That's cool. I've got a bag in the car from when I'm always crashing at Banks' place."

Adan stared at the tattooed, wide expanse of chest on display and nearly swallowed his tongue. Fuck. Nothing got him hotter than a strong man. Even the scary, somewhat demonic-looking ink heated his skin. To keep himself busy, Adan grabbed a fluffy towel.

"I'll get my bag and let you shower."

"Oh. You didn't want to join me?" He didn't know why he assumed Axton would. That had probably been a dumb thought after Adan turned him down last night. But they had talked about a lot of things, and Adan felt better about them now. He shouldn't have assumed Axton still wanted him. Plus, it was just a shower.

Rather than answer, Axton crowded his space and helped Adan out of his jacket and shirt. Adan couldn't look away from the intense way Axton watched him. The next thing Adan knew, his fingertips glided down Axton's sexy torso until they found Axton's belt. He worked it loose. His heart rate kicked up as he unbuttoned and unzipped Axton's pants. He wasn't scared. Adan was painfully turned on. The scary way Axton watched him was hot. He knew Axton was dangerous, but—for once—that deadly nature was on his side. The emotions focused on him were the exciting type of scary. He wanted more.

Axton's patience obviously snapped. Adan went from undressing Axton to sitting on the bathroom counter in a flash. Axton's tongue explored Adan's mouth. He kept one hand braced on the bathroom mirror while he held Adan in place with the other. Adan thought he might explode. Tiny sounds escaped him, and he wasn't even on Axton's cock yet.

"Oh god. Please don't stop." Adan didn't care that he begged. He had never been more certain he would die if he didn't get relief.

Axton peeled off his clothes. With Adan nude, he carried him to bed. From his spot on the mattress, he watched Axton disappear inside the bathroom. The sound of running water stopped. In no time, Axton was back. He dug through his wallet, coming out with a condom. His set expression had Adan beyond curious what thoughts ran through his head.

Adan motioned toward the bedside table. "There's lube in there."

If Axton heard, he didn't acknowledge the words. He stripped off the rest of his clothes. Adan's gaze ate up every inch of newly bared skin. He couldn't help but eye the same piercings he had fingered last night. Whoa. They were so much sexier than he expected. He squirmed at the idea of what they would feel like inside him.

"Don't be scared."

At the reassurance, Adan realized he hadn't stopped staring at Axton's dick. He met Axton's stare. "I'm not."

"Good." Axton grabbed his ankle and dragged him to the edge of the bed.

Adan fought the urge to yell "*whee*" and make the moment awkward. Then Axton worked on lubing Adan's asshole and all thought disappeared. Again, Axton manhandled him. He lifted Adan from the bed, leaving him no other choice but to straddle his lap when Axton sat in the wingback chair in the corner.

"I'm still covered in mud. I don't want to get your sheets dirty... yet."

Ho boy, Adan thought his head might explode. Axton was incredibly sexual. Adan wanted to taste him.

Axton handed him the condom. "I need to know you really want this."

Adan held his gaze and opened the condom with his teeth. He rolled it down Axton's length, going slow, and trying not to catch anything on a piercing. An unexpected nervous babble struck.

"I know you said the lip ring doesn't hurt, but this seems different." An uncomfortable-sounding chuckle burst from him.

Axton didn't laugh. He took Adan's hand and led it to his cock, stopping at the first ring—the one in his crown. "This one is all about sensitivity." He moved lower, hitting the next one. "This one is for you, and you'll know why soon." He moved to a different one on the other side of his dick. "This is for me. You can trust me."

He did. It was odd. He should recognize the hands of a murderer touched him, but Axton wasn't the first, and he was definitely the best. Adan shifted positions and slowly sank onto Axton's cock. He held the breath. Axton was huge. He knew the exact moment that piercing revealed its purpose. A moan burst from him with no permission from his brain. Holy shit. He had been unprepared. The ring hit the exact spot Adan craved.

Axton captured his mouth as he grabbed Adan's hips and took control. Adan turned to putty in his hands while Axton used him. He easily lifted and dropped

Adan, while surging upward and stealing Adan's soul. Adan had never felt fucked and made love to at the same time before. That was what happened now. Axton took him, but Adan swore he tasted his love. He felt cherished. The idea made his eyes burn while his body reveled in every thrust. Adan held Axton's face between his hands and savored every second of their kiss while Axton controlled his body. Adan fought his way toward the edge while also begging for the moment to never stop.

The pressure became too much. Adan tilted his chin back and tried dragging air into his lungs. His body moved closer and closer to what it craved. Axton sucked his neck, whispering praise against his skin. Adan couldn't understand a word. His pulse pounded too hard in his ears. The spring inside him snapped. Cries poured from him. Axton's thrust got harder. All Adan could do was shake in Axton's arms.

The words Axton babbled became clearer as his heart slowed. "Goddamn. You have no idea how much I've wanted you. Everything about you is perfect. You're way too good for someone like me. Why would you even let me touch you?"

Tears filled Adan's eyes. Axton truly thought he didn't deserve love. Maybe neither of them did, but goddamn it. Adan loved Axton.

He grabbed Axton's face and forced him to look him in the eyes. "I love you. You're perfect to me and I need to watch you blow."

For a moment, Axton looked ready to cry, and then he was on his feet. Adan's back hit the wall and Axton leaned into him so hard, Axton almost begged for another orgasm. He used the wall as leverage and fucked Adan. Axton wasn't gentle. He didn't let Adan hide. He held Adan's stare and took him. Without warning, another orgasm built and hit so fast it took his breath. An evil-looking smirk touched Axton's lips, fucking with Adan's head. Then Axton's expression hardened. His features turned terrifying, but he never looked away as he came. Adan knew the moment would burn into his memory. Later, he would take out the image and try to decide if he should be scared or thrilled. Either way, Adan wasn't going anywhere. This one was his.

Chapter Five

With hot water and bubbles surrounding him and Adan between his thighs, Axton had never been so content. He watched Adan play with a rubber duck. He squeezed the yellow toy, filling it with water before squeezing it again to spray water from his beak. Axton realized how much he enjoyed watching Adan savor a simpler life. He walked his fingers up Adan's spine, coaxing him into a better posture. Instead, Adan melted against his chest and squirted him over his shoulder.

A rumble of laughter escaped Axton. It sounded as tired as he was. "You honestly enjoy all this. It's not just an act."

It wasn't a question. Axton was pointing out the obvious. "Did you think I was putting on an act?"

Axton shrugged. "Not you in particular. I've spent a lot of time at The PlayPen and I'm a people watcher. It's crossed my mind several times that all this was some sort of mating dance for shared sexual fetishes. I don't know. That makes me sound judgmental. I'd just never encountered all this before my first visit to Banks' place."

"That's fair," Adan said, sounding like he truly wasn't insulted. "For some people, it might be some sort of strange mating dance. They have to put themselves on full display, so if they're approached by a daddy, that guy knows what he's in for. But for most, they're just being their true selves and hoping to be accepted. Take Soren, for example. He never went to The PlayPen looking for a daddy. He wanted a family."

"Yet he still found Shane."

A soft laugh fell from Adan's lips. "That was an accident, I think. They stumbled over each other. Maybe that makes for the best relationships. Neither of you is looking, and then there you are."

Oddly, that made perfect sense to Axton. He felt Adan shrug.

"As for me, I've always been alone. I've had to make my own happiness. Adult shit bores me."

"I assumed you were always under Beau's thumb." He hated saying Beau's name while he held Adan, but Axton wanted every detail of his life.

"I was, but then again, I wasn't. There was practically a whole wing for me in that crazy big house. I had a playroom with every toy imaginable. If I wanted anything, I got it. But Beau only visited me when he fought with Tabitha. He only dragged me from the room when he wanted to punish her or his boys by having me act as the happiest of playthings. Most of the time, I don't know what he did, but I didn't see him."

"That does sound lonely."

"Much like prison."

A bark of laughter burst from Axton at Adan's quip. "That's nothing like prison. You're never alone. It's never quiet. Not really. But it is still lonely, except you're constantly surrounded by people. Now, sometimes the quiet is too fucking quiet. I haven't slept without the TV on since I got home." He paused when he realized that wasn't completely true. "Unless I'm at Banks' place. Then I'm usually passed out from partying."

"Sometimes I think a wild life sounds kind of exciting." He could hear the smile in Adan's voice. "Then I think it sounds exhausting and scary. I mean, you actually let someone pierce your dick. That's crazy."

Axton laughed so hard, no sound emerged. His body shook. He tried to talk with no air. "You haven't even found them all yet."

Adan sat up and turned. He looked floored. "You're kidding. There's more? Where?"

While Axton managed to get his laugher under control, he couldn't stop smiling. "I take it you don't like all my accessories."

Adan blushed. "I didn't say that." He squirted Axton with the duck again. "How many did I miss?"

"Just one."

Adan narrowed his eyes. "Show me."

Axton plucked the duck from Adan's hand and set it aside. He took Adan's hand and slid it down his torso while holding Adan's stare. Axton held Adan's hand in place as he reached between his legs to the spot between his balls and asshole.

Adan's eyes widened. He toyed with the ring, making Axton bite back a moan. Adan cocked his head to one side and openly studied Axton's expression. "This turns you on."

Axton wasn't one to hide his desires. "What can I say? I love having my ass played with."

His confession seemed to embolden Adan. "Like this?" He pressed the tip of his finger against Axton's asshole, but he didn't penetrate him.

A shaky-sounding breath escaped Axton. "Yeah. Kind of like that."

"You should show me someday when I'm not so sore. It's been a really long time since I had sex."

Axton's eyebrows snapped together. "Why didn't you say something? I'd never hurt you."

A sweet smile touched Adan's lips. "Hush. I loved every second."

That appeased Axton a hair. "Still."

Adan's hand swept up Axton's semi hard cock. "You're not allowed to have regrets. That would hurt my feelings."

With Adan stroking him, Axton already forgot what they were talking about. "Okay. Whatever you want. It's yours." Axton would have agreed to anything. He didn't care as long as Adan didn't stop touching him. Axton snagged Adan's hips and hauled him into his lap, forcing Adan to straddle him. "Come here." He scooted forward at the same time as he pulled Adan closer against him, making their erections bump. He held them together and stroked.

Adan dropped his forehead to rest on Axton's shoulder, staring down at the space between their bodies. "Why is everything about you perfect for me?"

Axton's throat swelled at the question. Not necessarily for a good reason. "Why do you say that like you don't want it?"

Adan's head shot up. His fiery gaze met Axton's stare. "I want it. I want this. You. Please don't take it from me."

Axton realized Adan was every bit as desperate for whatever they were building. While holding Adan against him, he stood. He climbed from the tub and headed for bed, still soaked. Bubbles ran down their skin. Even he felt his intensity. Axton gently set Adan on the bed and followed him down. His mouth found Adan's lips. He rolled his hips, creating friction between them as he toyed with Adan's tongue. His eyes burned at the sweetness of the moment. Even with his body on fire, he felt more with his heart. No one had ever made him feel the way Adan did. He felt loved and accepted in a way he never had.

Adan's fingers linked with his. He held on like Axton was every bit as precious to him. If he lost this, Axton wouldn't survive it.

He had never kissed anyone who kissed like Axton. It was overwhelming, yet sensual. Even with his body ablaze, he focused on the way Axton savored him. His kiss was like Axton's way of making love. It was part of the act. Adan was here for every second. He never expected happiness to last. Life had taught him feeling good always got ripped away from him. Some people weren't destined to have good lives. Axton made him feel like he could stay this way forever.

Axton's light hair surrounded them. With the bathroom light shining through the locks, his hair looked almost white. He would age well. Adan hoped he was around to see that. His thoughts were all over the place, but Axton fucked with his head. They felt very real. Built on friendship. He was scared as hell of losing him.

The building pressure won. Adan turned his head and sucked air. He fought to blow. Adan wanted to fly. Pleasure was right there, calling his name. His body screamed for release.

Axton's sexy lips touched Adan's ear. "I love you."

The softly spoken words brushed Adan's heart, and his body jerked. A cry tore from his throat as Axton's thrusts sent him hurtling over the edge. Something needy burst from his soul. Axton had to feel the way he made Adan feel. It wasn't just love, but a crazed desperation to stay like this forever. Axton had to want him as badly as Adan wanted them.

He shoved at Axton's chest until he had Axton on his back. Adan kissed a path down Axton's body, dragging his tongue through his own cum. He had to feel those piercings on his tongue. Adan had to know how Axton tasted. It was agony knowing Axton hadn't come yet. Adan had to make him fly. He swallowed Axton's dick.

Axton's hips left the bed. "Holy shit." His fingers dove into Adan's hair. He didn't tug or force Adan in any way. It was like he needed to feel Adan's head bobbing on his cock. Adan let him have his wish. He had sworn to himself he would never be on his knees again. This wasn't the same. They were making love. This was love.

"Goddamn, Adan." A grunt escaped Axton, one that sent a sexy chill down

Adan's spine. He wanted Axton to make all the noises.

Adan tongued all the piercings Axton claimed were for his pleasure, including the one below his balls.

Axton writhed beneath him like Adan completely stole his senses. "I'm not going to survive. Fuck. That feels good." A loud groan rent the air. Hot cum filled Adan's mouth. Before he had time to swallow, he was ripped away. Axton had him pinned beneath him and his tongue explored Adan's mouth like he hunted for every hint of cum. The sexiness was nearly his undoing. Axton was so goddamn carnal. He was dangerous to Adan's heart and sanity. The thing about Adan was, he was stupid. As long as Axton kept showing up, Adan wouldn't turn him away. Any love at all was more than he deserved. He needed every drop.

CHAPTER SIX

AXTON WOKE UP TO a letter letting him know Adan had gone to work. Sunlight poured into the room and still Axton had slept like the dead. He stretched. A smile pulled at his lips. He could stay in bed all day, but he had things he wanted to do. It was time to deal with Beau so they could move on with their lives.

As much as it pained him to leave the warm bed that smelled like Adan, he did. He found his pants and ran out to his truck for his overnight bag. As usual, Axton went through the process of checking for trackers and explosives. While he didn't think Beau would try to blow up his vehicle for fear of Adan being with him, he absolutely believed Beau would track him. Axton didn't find anything suspicious. All he found was Adan's cat ears still inside the truck. He grabbed them and his bag.

Axton went through his morning routine, trying like hell to get the tangles out of his hair. He should probably cut it someday, but his hair was so fucking light, he already looked white-headed. When he had short hair, he looked like he was going bald. It was honestly kind of aggravating. Once he was clean and had his shit together, he locked up and then stashed his bag back in the truck. Axton circled the building. He couldn't leave without saying goodbye.

As Axton rounded the corner, a growl rose in his throat. Beau's SUV was parked near the door. He supposed this saved him from having to hunt the guy down. Still, a man could only tolerate so much. He didn't get Beau at all. Beau had built an empire from the ground up. The guy obviously wasn't weak or dumb. Yet when it came to emotions, the guy was a total dumbass. Likely, he was beyond all hope.

Axton didn't bother looking for Beau as he came through the door. His gaze automatically found Adan. Adan lit like a bonfire the second he spotted Axton. His expression warmed Axton's chest. He had never had this. Adan couldn't possibly understand what he gave Axton, but Axton would make sure Adan felt his love every day.

"Hey." Adan sounded breathless as he skipped to meet Axton.

"Hey." He held up the headband. "This was in the truck." Axton put it on for Adan. "There."

Adan touched the ears. "Thank you. I wondered where they had gone. You said they were in the truck. Are you going somewhere?"

"Yeah. I have a few errands to run, but I'll be back by the time your shift ends."

Adan bounced a little. "Okay. Be careful."

Without thinking about where they were, Axton cupped Adan's face between his hands. He swept a kiss across Adan's lips before giving him a peck on the nose.

Finally, he pressed his lips to Adan's forehead. "I love you. You be careful too." His gaze collided with Beau's stare over Adan's head. His face was expressionless, but his eyes looked cold and murderous.

"I love you too."

Adan's sweet claim brought Axton's attention back to him. "Text me if you need anything."

"Okay. Oh. That guy asked for coffee. Oops."

Axton smiled as he watched Adan bounce away. Then he focused on Beau. He became his realest self. Beau had once hired him to commit murder. Now he had to deal with the killer. He crossed the room. Beau watched his approach. In the corner of his vision, he saw two men move. Beau held up his hand.

Axton pressed his palms against the table and leaned Beau's way, keeping their conversation between them. "We have some bullshit to settle. I won't do that here and I sure as hell won't do it on your terms. Meet me at The PlayPen tonight at six. It's time for this shit to end."

Beau dipped his chin.

The PlayPen belonged to Banks. As Beau's youngest son, the place was neutral ground. Beau would never pull anything around Banks. Banks was crazy. Even his own father feared his wrath.

With a meeting in place, Axton walked away. The shit with Beau would end how it ended, but it would stop tonight. Axton wanted a future with Adan. A real one without Beau. He had to find a way to make that happen. Beau's sons seemed like the best place to start.

Adan was very careful putting himself together to go to The PlayPen with Axton. He understood Axton had no desire to be a daddy. Adan didn't want to embarrass him. He didn't own a lot of clothes, and what he owned all had coffee stains from work, so getting dressed was an exercise in frustration. Finally, he chose a dark purple T-shirt, hoping the stains wouldn't be as obvious. He didn't feel good about the choice. Adan didn't feel like himself at all.

Giving up, he stepped from the bathroom and tried to be an adult. "Okay. I guess I'm ready."

Axton's gaze swept down his body. His expression hid his thoughts. "Is that what you're wearing?"

Adan didn't want to cry, but he thought he might. He had already been so unsure and now Axton had proven his thoughts correct. "Maybe you should just go without me. Everything I own looks like this. I can't afford new clothes and I get coffee on everything while working." Even he heard the defeat in his voice.

From his spot on the couch, Axton eyed him, as if seeing him for the first time. Adan wasn't sure that was a good thing. He liked thinking Axton saw him through rose-colored glasses. Adan hated that was ending already. Axton made a dismissive gesture. "That's not what I meant. Why aren't you wearing your pajamas?"

"Oh." That was the last thing Adan expected. "I don't want to embarrass you."

A sweet smile touched Axton's lips. He stood and closed the gap between them. His lips swept across Adan's mouth. "You could never embarrass me, especially by just being you. Put on some pajamas. I have a surprise for you."

No matter how hard Adan tried to hide how ecstatic he was, he couldn't squash his smile. "Okay. Give me a second. I think I only have one pair clean. It's a lot of hard work, carting my clothes to the nearest laundromat." He darted inside his bedroom and dug through the dresser. There was a two-piece set with fire trucks. Adan didn't wear the outfit often because it was a little tight. The shirt had shrunk and showed off part of his stomach. But if Axton wanted him to wear pajamas, he would.

This time, when Adan emerged inside the living room, Axton wasn't expressionless any longer. When his gaze swept down Adan's body, heat flashed in his eyes. "This is my first time seeing this outfit. It definitely leaves nothing to the imagination." He met Adan's stare. "I like it." He waved Adan closer. "Come here."

Adan practically skipped to Axton.

Axton patted his lap. "Sit. I have something for you."

Adan climbed into Axton's hold. While sitting sideways across Axton's lap, he tried to hide his excitement. He loved surprises.

Axton shifted and pulled something fuzzy from beneath his thigh. "Put these on." He took Adan's hands and helped him slip on a pair of furry, fingerless cat paws. They were adorable.

Adan turned his hands from side to side, eyeing the little paw pads. He squealed. "They're so fucking adorable."

A sexy chuckle rumbled from Axton. "One more thing." He reached over the arm of the couch and grabbed something from the floor that sat out of sight. It was a helmet. It had cat ears.

Adan's mouth fell open. "Are you serious?"

Axton's grin proved how proud he was of the gift. "If you'll be riding with me all the time, you need your own helmet. Let's get it on you."

He managed to sit still long enough for Axton to get the strap adjusted. Adan was dying to look in the mirror. "How do I look?"

Axton's gaze moved over his face. "Like my gorgeous kitty."

Something inside Adan gave way. It didn't matter how Axton felt about being a daddy. Nothing mattered except being with this flawless person who made everything better. "Thank you."

"Don't thank me. I'm the one who gets to stare at you all adorable like this."

Adan shook his head. "Not for the gifts, even though they're amazing and thank you for those too, but thank you for this. For being here and not seeing me the way everyone else does. I don't deserve to have someone as amazing as you in my life, yet here you are. You'll never know how grateful I am."

Halfway through his speech, Axton's expression turned serious. "The fact that you think I'm worth anything at all is crazy to me. Don't thank me. I'm not sure I don't have an ulterior motive. I can't promise this isn't me bribing you to please keep loving me. The ability to do things with a conscience left me a long time ago. I'm just not sure of my actions anymore."

It hurt Adan's chest that Axton couldn't see that he was a good person. It was obvious no one had ever believed in him. He took off the helmet. "Take it back. Get your money back. I don't need gifts. I used to have everything. None of it meant a damn thing because I didn't have love. Now I do and I'm not losing it if I can help it. So don't bribe me."

Axton plopped the helmet back on Adan's head and strapped it on. "You're right. It's just stuff and I want you to have it all because I love you. Everything about you."

Even though Adan understood Axton tried to get a point across with his last statement, he refused to read too much into things. Adan was used to being whatever everyone else wanted. He would do the same for love.

"We should go." Axton stood, holding Adan as if he weighed nothing.

Adan snuggled close when it became obvious Axton had no plans to set him on his feet. He let Axton lock up his apartment and carry him down the stairs. Axton didn't set him down until they reached his bike. Then he stole a quick kiss before straddling the Harley and waiting for Adan to do the same. Adan crawled on behind him and held on. He didn't stop smiling the entire ride to The PlayPen. Something kept growing bigger between them. Adan had never felt more hopeful about his future, even while seeing no way out from beneath Beau.

At The PlayPen, Axton held his hand as they headed inside. For the first time, someone was proud to be seen with him. It felt amazing. Beau never held his hand.

Adan had always just sort of followed in his wake and existed in his shadow. Axton kept bringing Adan's hand to his mouth and kissing it. Each and every time, Adan's chest swelled.

Inside the play area, Adan scanned the room. The only Little he recognized was Beau's lawyer's husband, Luca. Luca always made a point of turning his back on Adan or leaving when Adan arrived. His shoulders fell at the idea of playing alone again.

"Is it okay if I sit with you?"

Axton didn't hesitate. "Of course, but I have a meeting first." His gaze swept over the tables where the daddies sat, as if searching for someone. "Here." Axton led him to an empty table. "How about this?" He pulled out a chair for Adan. "You sit here and play with this." Axton pulled out his phone and clicked around before setting the device on the table in front of Adan. "Smack the fish, kitty."

A bright smile lit Adan from the inside out when he saw the fish flying across the screen. He swatted one, and it went flying. A laugh burst from him. He smacked another one.

Axton kissed his ear. "I'll be right back, baby."

"Okay." He didn't watch Axton leave. Adan was too focused on getting all the fish.

"Hello, little one."

A chill ran down Adan's spine. His chin lifted. He subtly looked for Axton.

A knowing smile stretched Beau's lips. He held a bouquet of roses out to Adan. "Don't bother. I had one of my guards distract him. It's just us."

Only Beau would see every other person in the building as nothing or no one and consider them alone. In his eyes, they were. No one would dare stop him from doing whatever he wanted to Adan. A wave of sadness washed over Adan. This was one of Beau's biggest flaws. He didn't see people as people, even when they begged to be noticed. Adan didn't touch the flowers. Beau didn't need any encouragement.

"You have to stop this, Boo." The words fell from Adan, sounding as if they came from his soul. Adan couldn't stop. Beau looked like he didn't know how to react, and Adan took full advantage. "You already lost Tabitha. Now your boys are on their way out. It's time to stop."

Something flashed in Beau's eyes. "My boys will fall in line. They always do. They're both married now and have their own lives. There's no reason we can't start over."

Sadness weighed heavily on Adan. "Oh, Boo. There are a million reasons we can't start over. Do you really want Boone and Banks to simply fall in line? Don't you want your boys back? You have to stop using me as the weapon you bludgeon them with. It's time to just love your kids and find a way to fix things with them. For real this time. No manipulation. They used to really love you and look up to you. It's not too late to get that back, but it'll never happen if I go back home with you, and you know it. They'll never see me as anything other than that person who drove a wedge between Tabitha and you."

"You didn't."

A sad smile pulled at Adan's lips. "I certainly didn't help anything and all I can do at this point is destroy any chance you have left."

Beau leaned back in his seat. His dark gaze moved over Adan's face. "I'm pretty sure that ship has already sailed. Banks won't speak to me at all, and Boone sticks to business. At least you loved me. I think you're the only person who ever really has. How can you ask me to walk away?"

Adan took a deep breath. He knew Beau, probably better than anyone ever had. Beau never hid anything from Adan—the good or the bad. That was why Adan knew either Beau would listen now, or Adan would never be free. "I'm not asking. I'm telling you. Your sons lost their mother. Don't take away their dad."

A light tap landed on Adan's shoulder. He tore his gaze away from Beau. Luca stood, clutching a board game to his chest. "Would you like to play with me?"

Adan didn't even look to see what game he held. He scooped up Axton's phone and walked away, following Luca to a spot nearby on the floor. Adan didn't know what tomorrow would bring, but one way or another, Adan would never go back. Beau would never win, even if that meant Adan was dead.

So much bitterness, anger, and pain had sat on Beau's chest for so goddamn long. He hadn't known how to be human in a long time. While he had money and power, it brought him nothing. It simply funded and protected the addictions that destroyed his family. His rage at life had twisted him until he no longer knew what was real and what emotions he had manufactured to stop himself from killing everyone. He just wanted the pain to end. Beau no longer knew who he blamed or hated the most. All he knew was he couldn't stop punishing himself and everyone he loved. He needed them to feel his misery.

The bouquet of roses he had brought for Adan was suddenly swept away. An adorable blond boy, around the same age as Adan, clutched the flowers to his chest and spun.

"For me? Thank you. I love them." His blue eyes sparkled with mischief.

Despite everything, a smile tugged at Beau's lips. The guy was dressed crazy even for The PlayPen. He wore policeman pajamas with a pink tutu. A crown sat crooked on his head. His chaos was oddly charming.

Beau pulled out the teddy bear he hid beneath the table. He had wanted to surprise Adan. Adan didn't want him anymore. That was pretty typical of everyone he loved. "It comes with a bear if I can have a name."

"I thought you had a name. The kitty called you Boo."

Oh. He was a brat. Beau's smile grew. He shook the bear at his new friend.

The guy's gaze dropped to the stuffed animal. He obviously wanted it more than he wanted to be a smart ass. "Kylo."

With a dip of his chin, Beau handed Kylo the bear. "Just promise you'll think of me when you look at it."

Kylo's fingers closed around the bear's arm. His gaze never wavered from holding Beau's stare. He clutched the bear against his chest. "You have to think of me too." He set the flowers and bear on the table and took off his crown. Kylo moved in close and placed the crown on Beau's head. Up close, he was flawless. His light blue eyes were like the sky in the summer. With the crown in place, he met Beau's stare. "There. Now you can think about me every time you rule the kingdom, King Boo."

Goddamn. Beau was fascinated. There was no way Kylo knew who he was. There wasn't an ounce of fear in his eyes. Before Beau regained his wits, Kylo grabbed the flowers and bear and danced away. For much longer than necessary, Beau watched him twirl around the room. He caught sight of his guard. With a sigh, Beau stood. They were obviously having trouble with Axton. Maybe he should just hire Axton to take their place. The guy was obviously braver than them.

Beau headed for the foyer. When he turned the corner, he found Axton waiting, looking irritated.

When Axton spotted Beau, his eyes flashed with rage. "Did you have your guards keeping me waiting for you out here so you could harass Adan?"

Beau barely spared him a glance, instead focusing on his guards. The men obviously tried hard not to stare at Beau's newly acquired crown. Beau owned it. It was a gift from someone who saw him at his lowest and saved him. He nodded toward the door. "Let's go. This is over."

Rico looked Axton's way before meeting Beau's stare again. He licked his lips nervously. Yeah. Beau should just hire Axton. "What about him?"

"This is over," Beau repeated. He headed for the door without looking back. His guards scrambled to stay ahead to open the door for him. Beau had expected his pride to sting at the idea of bowing out, but he felt nothing. Adan was right. It was time to stop. He didn't want to lose his boys. That meant he had to find a better way.

CHAPTER SEVEN

WHILE AXTON HADN'T KNOWN what his meeting with Beau would bring, he never thought Beau would simply bow out. Considering Axton had left Adan in the playroom and that was where Beau had appeared from after a considerable wait, Axton knew Adan had to be the reason Beau chose to quit. He waited until Beau left before heading back to the playroom. His eyes automatically landed on the table where he had left Adan. For a moment, his heart stopped. Had Beau harmed Adan? Was that why he looked so calm about leaving? Axton's gaze frantically bounced around the room. He spotted his brother first. Jarek rested on his side on the floor next to Luca. Axton nearly dropped in relief when he saw Adan with them. He was all smiles. A wave of love washed over Axton. Not just for Adan, but also for his brother, who had obviously kept Axton's heart safe in his absence. As quickly as the love hit, the shame set in. Jarek always watched his back, even when Axton didn't ask for it or notice. Maybe even more so in those times. He wasn't like the people who raised them. Jarek loved him.

Axton crossed the room.

Jarek's gaze met his as he approached.

"Thank you." Axton silently mouthed the words.

Jarek dipped his chin.

Axton reached Adan's side just in time to catch Adan showing Luca the fish game. He passed Luca a kitty paw. "Go ahead. I know Daddy won't mind."

Axton's throat swelled. His feet froze.

Adan startled as he noticed Axton. A bright red blush exploded across his face. "Sorry." He winced. "It's a habit."

A huge realization struck Axton. He didn't care. Axton joined him on the floor and stole a quick kiss. "It's fine, baby. I fell in love with all of you. Don't change."

Adan's bright smile was everything. While Axton wasn't totally sure what he had just agreed to do, he had faith in them. He had known Adan's personality since day one. He genuinely wouldn't change anything about him.

With a deep breath for courage, Axton focused on Jarek. "How have you been?"

Jarek smiled. He looked hopeful. "I've been good. How about you?"

Axton fought the urge to look Adan's way. "I've been really good." He cleared his throat. "So, I've been thinking—"

"Luca showed me a picture of all these amazing Lego sets they've put together. They have a Lego room and everything. He says I can come help, if I want. Can we go?"

Even though Adan looked hopeful, Axton fully recognized Adan had interrupted him to save him. He had kept Axton from swallowing his pride to rebuild the relationship with his brother.

He met Jarek's stare. "I'd love that."

Jarek's expression made Axton's throat swell. He realized—hopefully, not too late—that he had a family. Jarek looked hopeful, yet scared of getting crushed. Until that moment, Axton hadn't noticed what he put Jarek through with his rejections and life decisions. While Axton had a lot of regrets, every move he made through life had led him to Adan. He wouldn't know this current happiness without his past fuck-ups. That didn't mean he couldn't start fresh. The problem was that would never happen if they didn't confront the past. This wasn't the place or time, but Axton was afraid he might lose his nerve.

"Your dad wasn't my dad."

Jarek stayed completely expressionless, despite the sudden confession.

Adan shuffled closer.

Axton pulled him into his lap and continued. He needed to hold Adan for strength. "That's what they were fighting about the night they died and that's why I just wasn't loved the way you were."

Jarek's chest expanded as he took a deep breath. He slowly released it. "I know and I'm sorry I didn't realize it back when it mattered. We were given all the same things, and I had my head buried in my goals. You deserved better from everyone, especially me. You're my brother. Not a half sibling or unwanted responsibility. You're my brother. I love you. Nothing else matters."

Axton couldn't speak. His throat was too swollen. He nodded and cleared his throat. "I love you too."

Adan squeezed his hand.

Axton automatically kissed his ear. The truth sank in. It was Adan's love that set him free and opened his eyes. He had let go of so much when he chose to make room for Adan. If Adan and he could see the best in each other when everyone else only saw the worst—and there was a lot of worst to see—then Axton could look past his childhood trauma to reach for his brother. Nothing that happened to Axton over the years was because of Jarek. While Jarek might have been oblivious to a lot of things, he wasn't cruel, and he loved Axton.

Luca passed Adan back his paw and Axton's phone. He crawled Jarek's way. "I'm hungry, Daddy. Can we get pizza?"

Jarek sat up and pulled Luca into his arms. "Of course, baby." He looked Axton's way. "How about it, guys? Would you like to get some pizza? We can eat while we check out the Lego room."

Adan looked his way with hope bleeding from his eyes.

Axton squeezed him and stood with a giggling Adan tucked under one arm. "Sounds great. We'll follow you."

Luca covered his mouth and stifled a laugh over Adan's predicament.

Jarek stood and tossed Luca over his shoulder. "After you."

They exchanged smiles, and it was as if the clouds parted. He was happy. Truly content deep in his heart. Beau had backed down, and he had his brother back. Adan had called him Daddy. Life was going places.

With his heart and stomach full, and Axton's giant nude body curled around him, Adan had never been more content. Axton's bed was ridiculously cozy. Adan wished he could sleep like this—in Axton's arms—every night. He wouldn't start that hope, only to be crushed. Life never took mercy on him for long.

"What happened with Beau?" Axton massaged Adan's hip as he asked the question, as if worried he might send Adan running or ruin the moment.

Adan smiled into the dark. He found peace in these intimate moments where they calmly spoke like a real couple. No yelling or fighting. No judgment. "He tried to give me flowers."

Axton snorted. "You don't even like flowers. You're allergic."

Adan's smile grew. "Just more proof he never loved me. This entire stalking thing has been about pride or loneliness. Both. I don't know, but it had nothing to do with me. Still, I don't really know what happened. He set those roses on the table, and I looked into his eyes. Everything went sort of calm inside me and I just kind of started talking. I didn't make it about me or about rejection. Instead, I made it about him and reclaiming what was left of his family. Then Luca saved me from the conversation, and I don't know. Next I looked, he was gone. What about you? What happened on your end?"

He felt Axton shrug. "He said it was over." Adan's eyes fell closed. A weight lifted from his chest. When he spoke with Beau, things felt different. Calmer. For once, he thought Beau listened, but hearing Axton confirm his thoughts felt amazing and also a little sad. A chapter closed in his life. It was a long chapter too. He had been part of the Bosi family for longer than he had been an adult. Now he was officially an orphan.

Axton ran his fingers through Adan's hair. "Are you okay, baby?"

Adan chewed his bottom lip. His eyes stung. It was so stupid. He wanted to be free of Beau. Adan definitely didn't want Axton to think Adan wanted anyone else. "I'm alone in the world." The words fell in a whisper that came from his soul. Adan hadn't meant to speak. It was Axton. Adan could never stop himself from telling him everything. "I guess I have been for a long time." But it felt very real tonight. Axton had reconnected with his brother. Adan wasn't stupid. He knew the only reason anyone had been nice to him lately was because of Axton and maybe a little for Soren's sake. Adan was still the most hated boy in town. He felt very weak and exposed tonight for seemingly no reason at all. Sometimes, reality hit from nowhere and the bed he had made was swallowing his sanity whole.

"So, am I only your daddy sometimes? I'm confused. I'm new to this."

A sad smile tugged at Adan's lips. He loved Axton so much. No one tried as hard as him. "It's okay. I know that's not a role you want. This is just a bad moment for me. Sometimes reality just smacks me in the face. I'll be fine. I love us the way we are."

Axton gently urged Adan on to his back. With his weight braced on one elbow, Axton stared down at him. "Call me Daddy."

He sounded so serious and a little angry. "Okay. Like, right now?"

"Yes."

Adan was confused as fuck, but he did as told. "Okay, Daddy."

A small growl vibrated from the back of Axton's throat. His hand swept down Adan's body before diving beneath him and roughly squeezing Adan's ass. "Mean it."

A pant escaped Adan at the heat in Axton's voice. "Daddy."

"Damn right," Axton said, sounding gruff. "You're mine." He shifted positions, crawling between Adan's thighs. Adan heard the lube tube open and close above his head. Then Axton's wet fingers probed his hole. Adan drew his knees higher, giving him free access. "This little asshole is mine." Before Adan could react, Axton impaled him. Adan hadn't been prepared for the huge intrusion. Neither did he have time to tense. He gasped for air. Axton took full advantage. He grabbed Adan's face and his tongue shoved inside Adan's mouth. Adan couldn't keep up.

Axton pulled away, but didn't release his hold. He pumped inside Adan. "All of you belongs to me. How dare you say you have no one? You have me."

Adan realized too late how he must have sounded to Axton. They were ridiculously co-dependent. For over a year, they had leaned on each other and fell in love. They knew each other like no one else did. If the shoe was on the other foot, and Axton said he had no one, Adan would be brokenhearted. Axton had him.

"I'm sorry, Daddy. I didn't mean to hurt you. You're my everything." He stroked Axton's face.

Axton's hold softened. His mouth covered Adan's. This time, his kiss was loving and melted Adan's heart. "I love you, kitty," he whispered between kisses.

Adan's eyes filled with tears even as his body burned. Axton was so strong. It was easy to forget how much he needed Adan too. "I wish I could make love to you and make you see how crazy in love I am with you. Nobody has ever owned my heart like this."

Axton froze. He pulled away enough to meet Adan's stare. "Are you being serious?"

Adan didn't know how to respond. Even though he had spoken in the heat of the moment, he meant his words. He couldn't read Axton to see if he should take them back. Ultimately, he wanted them to always be honest with each other. "Yes." Heat crawled up Adan's cheeks.

"I mean, I've never actually done that, and I don't even know if I'd like it, but you make me feel ways I never have before. It sounds insane, but I want to crawl under your skin to be closer to you. I can't explain it. I just want you in every way."

Thankfully, Axton didn't laugh at him. In fact, he looked downright horny, but they were in the middle of making love, so that was fair. Axton licked his lips. He looked nervous, almost as if he expected to be rejected. "I could walk you through things."

Adan had only been partially serious, but his dick suddenly wept at the idea. His lust climbed to a new level. "You wouldn't mind trying that?"

A sexy smirk stretched Axton's lips. "Baby, I'm vers. I love to get fucked."

"Oh." Adan had never thought to ask about Axton's preferences. He had assumed by Axton's overwhelming manliness that he wouldn't be down for that. But it also wasn't like Adan had seen himself craving such a thing.

Axton's expression turned serious. "Don't worry. If you don't like it, I'm good. This is real love. You're who I want to be with for the rest of my life. Even if we never had sex again, I'd still choose you over anyone else."

God. Adan had done nothing to deserve this man. Everyone knew it. The universe knew it. But Adan wouldn't let Axton get away. He would do whatever it took to make him happy. "I'm not worried about liking it. It's you. Everything about you turns me on. I don't want to disappoint you."

Axton pulled out and found the lube again. "Then how about I just use you, baby boy?"

Holy shit. Adan had never wanted to be inside anyone. He did now. Adan was more than a little concerned he wouldn't last ten seconds. Just the idea of Axton using him had him half insane already. He watched Axton lube them. Adan gripped the sheets beneath him, trying to stay grounded. Then Axton grabbed Adan's cock, held it in place, and sank onto him.

The moan that vibrated from Axton had Adan losing sight in one eye. The sudden heat surrounding his dick tested his will like nothing ever had before. Then Axton did exactly as he claimed he would. He used Adan. Adan tried to keep up, but everything felt too good. His brain wouldn't work.

"Mmm. Damn, baby boy, you feel fucking amazing. It's like you were made just for me."

Adan couldn't make a sound. His back teeth were locked to keep him from immediately blowing.

"I can't wait for you to pump me full of cum. I want to feel your juices leaking from my ass."

Holy shit. Adan was going to die. Axton's long hair stuck to his sweaty face as he rode Adan's body. Adan stared up at him and watched the show. Axton obviously had the angle he needed. His expression was the sexiest porn Adan had ever seen. This overly pierced and tattooed bad boy looked like he would die without Adan's cock. Adan was mesmerized and more aroused than he had ever been in his entire life. He was taking good care of his daddy. Pride swelled his chest and unshed tears burned his eyes. He thought he had been in love before Axton. Adan wasn't as sure now. He had never felt like this. Adan could never hurt Axton the way he had others in the past. He'd rather die.

"You're so beautiful, Daddy. Can I marry you?"

A cry tore from Axton. Cum arced through the air and hit Adan's chest. The sudden convulsions of Axton's asshole caught Adan by surprise. He gasped as an unexpected orgasm slammed into him. Adan had tried so hard to hold back that the surprise blow was twice as power-ful as he expected. His body jerked and then shook. Sounds came from him with-out his control. He didn't try to stop them. Adan's brain no longer worked. His system was too busy glitching as his dick spit, filling Axton's ass. They had never really discussed sex without condoms. But Adan knew inmates were regularly tested and Adan had been too. A childhood like his would do that to a person. Right now, though, life was fucking flawless. His body hummed with pleasure. Axton's mouth covered his and their tongues played. He felt the way Axton shook. Adan had never been so high on life. He didn't want to come down.

Axton's mind was all over the place. When he had realized he wanted Adan and was actually in love with the guy, he hadn't imagined any of this. Honestly, he had secretly thought they would flounder for a while before they figured out a way to navigate Axton's monstrous desires and Adan's kinks, which he imagined wouldn't match in any way, shape, or form. Yet here they were with Axton sitting on Adan's cock and with Adan's marriage proposal ringing in Axton's ears. Surely he hadn't meant it. Most likely, Adan's words had been heat of the moment ramblings. But Axton couldn't stop thinking about it, and he needed to know.

He nipped at Adan's bottom lip, keeping him slightly distracted while dealing with such a heavy topic. "Did you mean it about marrying me?"

As if Adan saw his game for what it was, Adan cupped his face, forcing him to be still and hold his stare. "I always mean everything I say to you. You're the love of my life." Adan licked his lips, turning visibly nervous. "I know I'm not that great of a catch or anything. Like I have literally nothing to offer."

Axton kissed him, cutting off that bull-shit. He pressed his forehead against Adan's, trying to absorb more of the love he had been starved of his entire life. "You're everything I need." Even Axton heard the way his voice broke. He swallowed. "If you'd seriously marry me and let me keep... all this, I'd give you the world. You'd never want for anything or shed a single tear. I swear I'd make you happy."

"You don't have to convince me. I'm the one who asked."

Despite the humor in Adan's voice, Axton still thought he might cry. There was no way Adan understood what his offer meant to Axton. No one had ever made him feel this wanted, especially in any sort of healthy way. They were solid and good. He genuinely believed they only wanted the best for each other in life. Axton had never had this.

Axton swallowed past the lump in his throat. "Okay. Let's do it."

"Yay." Adan's whispered cheer sounded how Axton felt—like emotions were too high for his throat to work. He heard Adan swallow, as if it hurt. "Your family and friends will be disappointed in you. I'm not who they'd choose for you."

"If anyone can't accept you, then they're not my family or friends. But I think you're wrong. People see you clearer than you realize."

Adan's body shook with silent laughter. "That's probably worse."

A smile exploded across Axton's face. He recognized it came from his soul. The night he had rescued Adan from the front steps of Beau's house was the best decision he had ever made. Too many times to count, he wished he had brought Adan home with him that night rather than leaving him at The PlayPen. They might have reached this place sooner. None of that mattered now, though. Axton planned to give Adan the brightest of futures. It would always be them against the world. That sounded like the greatest of fates to him.

Chapter Eight

WITH HIS HEART IN his throat, Adan twisted his fingers as he waited for his knock to be answered. As he shifted from foot to foot, Axton squeezed his shoulders. Axton knew him. That was more comforting than the squeeze. Adan didn't have to explain himself. They were a team. The door swung wide, and Shane smiled at the sight of them.

"Hey, guys. You haven't been around in a while."

Adan twisted his fingers again.

Axton sounded happy behind him. "Us? Every time we stop by, you guys are traveling."

Shane brightened even more. "That's true. Come in."

Adan stayed quiet, but followed Shane. He had only been inside Banks' place once. Adan had a feeling he had only been accepted that day because he had been with Soren and they had wanted Soren to have some time alone with Shane. As they stepped inside, Adan spotted Soren. He gave a tiny wave, unsure of his welcome. They hadn't seen each other in months. As Axton had said, Banks' bunch were always traveling.

Soren popped from the couch. "Adan!" He skipped across the room and hugged him, warming Adan's chest. Soren held him away and eyed his outfit. "You look so cute. You're like a biker kitty."

Adan flashed Axton a smile. They shared a moment. Axton kept buying him things that met him halfway. It was Little-esque in his leather kitty suit, but he also matched Axton's style. Adan had to admit they looked good together, and Adan felt adorable.

"You look like you belong on the back of Axton's bike," Kyson said, drawing Adan's attention toward the couch where Kyson sat with Banks.

"That's because that is where he belongs."

Banks looked thoughtful as he looked between them at Axton's comment.

Thankfully, Axton didn't force Adan to start the conversation. "So we kind of need to talk to you guys about something." Axton looked Soren's way. "I think Adan wants to ask you something first."

Adan worked up a grateful smile, even though he was nervous as hell. Soren looked curious, and Adan forced his throat to work. "Other than Axton, you're the only person I have. I know you've only been nice to me out of pity, and I'm probably not someone you consider a friend."

"That's not true, Adan." Soren sounded genuinely hurt by the claim.

Adan made a dismissive motion. "It's okay. I understand. It's my fault."

"It's not," Banks said, cutting off Adan's speech again. There was no mistaking the outrage in Banks' voice. It was beyond obvious Beau was the only person Banks blamed. Still, Adan knew better. He didn't deserve Banks' support.

Unfortunately, their interruptions were undermining Adan's confidence. He didn't know if he could finish his question.

Adan's gaze shot Axton's way. He was ready to cry. Adan shifted from foot to foot. He didn't want to ask for help, but he wasn't sure he had made the right decision. "Maybe I shouldn't."

Soren, being the kind soul he always was, took Adan's hands, pulling Adan's gaze back to him. His eyes were kind. "It's okay, Adan. I know I've been traveling a lot and I haven't kept in touch like I should. That's my fault. I got caught up in being a newlywed, but you are my friend and I'm sorry I made you feel otherwise. It won't happen again."

Adan took a shaky breath. He had been right to come here. They were friends. "Will you walk down the aisle with me?"

Soren blinked. "What?"

Adan rushed to explain. "I don't have anyone else, and I'd love to have you by my side when I marry Axton."

A rumble of surprised congratulations went around the room. Adan somewhat overheard Axton asking Banks to stand up with him, but he was too busy staring at Soren with all the hope in his heart. He didn't want to be alone for this.

Soren wore a huge grin. "I would love to. Just let me know when. I'm definitely there."

Adan took a deep breath. "Well, is today okay, then? We're kind of on our way there now."

Soren looked taken aback, but he didn't stop smiling. "Of course. Um." He looked around. "I don't know what to wear or anything. I have a suit I wore to my sister-in-law's wedding. Maybe that'll work?"

"Grab your favorite pjs."

Soren looked Axton's way and then back at Adan. "Yeah. Okay. Just give me a minute." He glanced toward Shane. "Oh. Is Shane invited?"

Adan jumped. "Oh. Ha. Sorry. Yes. Everyone is invited. I'm sorry. I forgot to say
that." To his shock, everyone was all
smiles and looked excited to join him.
Adan knew it was so much more than
he deserved and more than likely Axton
they actually supported. But it meant a
lot to him that they wouldn't be alone
on their wedding day. Of course, Jarek
and Luca would be there, but they were
only there for Axton. Adan literally had
no one.

Soren grabbed his hand and dragged
him into a different room. Adan glanced
around. It was obviously Soren and
Shane's bedroom. "Tell me everything."
He dug around for pajamas while Adan
grappled for words.

"Besides you guys, it's only Jarek and
Luca. Well, plus Wrecker and his hus-

band, Johnny. Johnny is ordained, so he's going to marry us." A bright smile lit Adan's face. "We're marrying on the roof of the Back Porch. That's where Axton and I fell in love."

Soren cooed. "That's so sweet, but I guess I meant for you to tell me about Axton and you. I didn't even know you two talked, much less were together."

Adan's cheeks heated. "Yeah. Like you said, you've been traveling a lot. I don't know if you knew this, but he's the one who brought me here the night Beau kicked me out. Afterward, he kind of kept coming around. Then when I moved to the apartment, he kept coming even more often. We spent a lot of time talking." Adan's hands rose and fell. "We were completely open with each other and neither of us judged. I don't know. We just clicked—like we had always been meant to be together." Adan pressed his hands against his hot cheeks. "I've never been this happy, Soren. He knows me better than anyone ever has, and he loves me anyhow." Adan's throat swelled and his eyes filled with tears. "He's so much more than I'll ever deserve."

Soren crossed the room and hugged him. "Stop. You deserve this. I really wish you would talk to someone sometime—like a professional—so they can make you understand who was really to blame in your life."

Adan didn't want to have this conversation. Not on his wedding day, but he wanted Soren to see him as he was. He placed his hands on Soren's shoulders and held him away enough to hold his stare. "Please don't completely paint me as the victim. There were a lot of years when I loved Beau. There were a lot of years I prayed he would get divorced and choose me."

A sweet smile touched Soren's lips. "Of course you did. You're human and he was all you had. But one day, you'll look back and realize that's exactly what Beau wanted by isolating you. If you didn't have anyone else and everyone hated you, then you'd be completely dependent and beholden to him. You'd have nowhere to go and no one to turn to for help. You'd see him as your everything because he literally was everything. Beau was an adult, playing adult games with someone who wasn't mature enough to understand and then he kept you from growing past that emotionally immature state. One day, you'll see all that and it'll piss you off."

A surprised bark of laughter burst from Adan. "Maybe, but—right now—I don't care about any of that. I'm happy for real for once."

Soren smiled. "Good. Then let's get you married."

Adan hugged him and bounced a little. "I'm so fucking excited."

Soren laughed and hugged him back. "Axton is a great guy. You'll have a fantastic life."

Adan believed it. Axton was amazing and gorgeous and perfect. Adan couldn't wait to be his husband. The past was exactly that—the past. He wouldn't let Beau or the memory of him ruin this amazing day.

Adan was about to marry his best friend. Literally nothing else mattered.

Not once in Axton's life had he considered or saw himself getting married. Just two years ago, he had fully believed he would die in prison. By old age or violently, he never thought he would leave that place, much less have any dreams for himself. If he had possessed enough hope to fantasize, he couldn't have imagined someone like Adan. Adan was so unique, there was no chance Axton could make him up in his head. He was too perfect for Axton. They matched in all the best ways.

Axton stood across from his best friend and said his vows with his whole chest. He loved this man. When it was over, a weight slipped from Axton's shoulders. They shared a smile that matched the overwhelming happiness in Axton's heart before their lips met. He barely heard the clapping as he held Adan as tightly as possible. Bubbles were blown in their faces as they headed for the ladder. Inside the coffee shop, Wrecker had closed for the day and one of his friends had set up a nice reception and baked them a gorgeous wedding cake. Everything felt surreal—like he watched someone else's life unfold. People spoke to him. Axton barely heard a word and forgot what was said the moment they moved away. Life didn't snap back into focus until he saw Jarek pull Adan aside.

His brother's too serious expression immediately lit a familiar rage. He wouldn't have the one good thing he had destroyed.

Axton inserted himself into the discussion. He draped his arm over Adan's shoulders and focused on Jarek with a bright smile. "What's up? Am I interrupting something?"

Jarek looked a tad guilty. "I hate to do this at your wedding, but it's unavoidable." He pulled an envelope from his inside pocket and held it out to Adan. "This is for you."

Adan looked as confused as Axton felt. He broke the envelope's seal. There was a letter inside. Adan cast him a worried look before pulling out the papers inside and unfolding them. Axton moved to read over his shoulder.

Baby Boy,

I know you think I'm heartless and I never considered you.

The papers shook slightly in Adan's hand. Axton half expected Adan to toss them aside. He didn't, so Axton kept reading.

That's not true. Before you, I never thought a person could love two people equally at the same time. I didn't want to love you. Being with you was supposed to be about shaking Tabitha from her addictions and forcing my son to stop acting so goddamn spoiled. People are supposed to fear me. I'm not soft. Never could I have dreamed how far my actions would push them. Yet, through it all, you never treated me like the monster I am. Not even now when it's so fucking obvious to everyone that I'm not good. You still speak to me like I'm human. You didn't deserve another predator. For that and a million other things, I'm so goddamn sorry.

Axton was blown away by that. He didn't see Beau as someone who apologized. Then again, Axton was sure Adan had seen a lot of things with Beau no one else ever had.

When I lost Tabitha and my sons, you were the only person I had left to punish. Coming out on the other side of things, I see every misstep I ever made. But when it comes to you, it was real. My love was genuine, as much as a psychopath can love anyone, anyhow. None of it is on you. You were just in the wrong place at the right time. I can't take our years back and I wouldn't even if I could. Like my sons, you're one of the only good pieces of me. So, like my sons, I need to know you're okay. Attached is a statement of accounts set up in your name. There are several to make them as legal as possible. Jarek will represent those accounts for you. No charge to you, of course. Don't turn these down, Baby Boy. They are well and legally in your name, which comes with a tax responsibility, so enjoy the life these funds provide. You earned it.

Love always,

Boo

Adan turned the page and swayed on his feet. Luckily, Axton was there to keep him upright.

"Oh my god."

Jarek remained professional. "Unfortunately, you don't have the luxury of saying no. The IRS doesn't give a fuck about anyone's pride. I'll make sure they're kept happy, but this amount of money is obviously life-changing." His gaze moved to hold Axton's stare. "Don't let this change how you feel about each other. Everyone standing here knows this money is deserved."

Adan sniffed. He handed the papers to Axton. "I don't even know what to do with any of this right now."

Axton refolded everything and stuck it in his back pocket. "It doesn't change anything about today and there's nothing we can't figure out together."

Adan stared at him with all the trust in the world. He always made Axton feel larger than life. "Let's buy you a new Harley."

A surprised bark of laughter burst from Axton. Of all the things he expected Adan to say, that wasn't it. "My Harley isn't that old."

Adan nodded. He looked thoughtful. His gaze slid Jarek's way. "Do you ride? I could buy you one and I could get one of those three-wheel things and decorate it so that it looks like a kitty. Oh, and I could get Luca one too and we could become like a family of bikers. What should we call ourselves?"

By the time Adan finished, Jarek and Axton roared with laughter.

Luca creeped closer, looking unsure of his welcome. "Is the business part over?"

Jarek snagged Luca's waist and tucked him against his side. He kissed Luca's temple.

Adan relayed his idea to Luca. "I was telling them I want to buy us all bikes so we can become a family biker gang. Except I'd get us those three-wheeled things that are easier to drive. Mine can look like a cat and yours can look like it's made of Legos."

Luca's eyes widened. "That sounds so cool. I don't know if I'd be brave enough to do that, but I can definitely picture you as a kitty biker."

Axton and Jarek exchanged glances. Huge grins exploded across their faces. That was the moment Axton knew his relationship with his brother would be fine and his future brighter than the sun.

He had the perfect husband and the life he hadn't known he needed. There was no way Axton could have pictured this for himself, but damn. He wouldn't have existence any other way.

Keep an eye out for the next Little Lost, *King Daddy.*

About the Author

CHARITY PARKERSON IS AN award-winning and multi-published author with several companies. Born with no filter from her brain to her mouth, she decided to take this odd quirk and insert it in her characters. One of her greatest loves is writing morally gray characters. You'll find them scattered throughout her hundreds of titles.

*Nine-time Readers' Favorite Award Winner

*2015 Passionate Plume Award Finalist

*2013 Reviewers' Choice Award Winner

*2012 ARRA Finalist for Favorite Paranormal Romance

*Five-time winner of The Mistress of the Darkpath

Connect with her online:

*Sign up for her newsletter: https://bit.ly /charityparkersonnewsletter

*Join her readers' group on Facebook: http://bit.ly/CharitysTribe

*Website: https://www.charityparkerso n.com

*A list of her social media accounts and giveaways all in one place: http://hy.pag e/charityparkerson

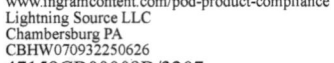